LUCKY ME,

LUCY McGEE

LUCKY ME,
LUCY MCGEE

BY
MARY AMATO

ILLUSTRATED BY
JESSICA MESERVE

HOLIDAY HOUSE   New York

Text copyright © 2020 by Mary Amato
Art copyright © 2020 by Jessica Meserve
All Rights Reserved
HOLIDAY HOUSE is registered in the U.S. Patent and Trademark Office.
Printed and bound in March 2020 at Maple Press, York, PA, USA.
First Edition
1 3 5 7 9 10 8 6 4 2
www.holidayhouse.com

Library of Congress Cataloging-in-Publication Data

Names: Amato, Mary, author. | Meserve, Jessica, illustrator.
Title: Lucky me, Lucy McGee / by Mary Amato ; illustrated by Jessica Meserve.
Description: First edition. | New York : Holiday House, [2020] | Summary:
"While Lucy McGee tries to track down her missing ukulele, the members of
the Songwriting Club must decide if it's worth competing against one
another in a giveaway for free concert tickets"— Provided by publisher.
Identifiers: LCCN 2019012139 | ISBN 9780823443642 (hardcover)
Subjects: | CYAC: Luck—Fiction. | Lost and found possessions—Fiction.
Clubs—Fiction. | Contests—Fiction.
Classification: LCC PZ7.A49165 Luc 2020 | DDC [Fic]—dc23
LC record available at https://lccn.loc.gov/2019012139

ISBN: 978-0-8234-4525-7 (paperback)

For all the singers, uke players, students,
teachers, and friends who make music
with Carpe Diem Arts — M. A.

CONTENTS

Chapter One

WHERE COULD YOU BE, UKULELE?

"Mom!" I yelled. "Have you seen my uke?"

My mom tapped me on the shoulder. "I'm right behind you, Lucy. You don't have to yell."

"Sorry!" I hurried past her and looked behind the couch.

"Don't tell me you lost your ukulele," she said.

"Remember what we talked about?"

I stopped.

Last month I lost my favorite hat. Last week I lost my homework. Last night I lost a library book. I said it was bad luck. My mom said it wasn't about luck, it was about paying attention. She had to say it three times because I wasn't paying attention. Then she said if I didn't get better at paying attention, she'd lose her mind.

I had to find my uke!

"It's probably in my room," I said. I smiled, even though I was worried. I had already looked in my bedroom. And in the bathroom. And in every other room in the house. No uke.

"Breakfast, Lucy!" my dad called from the kitchen. "It's almost time for school!"

My mom said goodbye and left for work.

"Keep an eye on Lily while you eat," my dad told me, and then he went to the basement to get a new sponge. I plopped down in my chair and ate a bite of cold toast. Lily sat in her high chair and stuck her fingers in the jelly jar and then licked them.

"Lily, that's gross," I said, and moved the jar away. "Where did Leo go?"

She pointed under the table. "Tutta."

Tutta is Lily's word for turtle, which meant that my brother had turned himself into a turtle again.

I looked under the table. There he was, all curled up, eyes closed.

"What's wrong with you?" I asked. Usually Leo turns himself into a turtle when he's sad or mad.

He didn't answer.

"I'm having a bad morning, too," I whispered. "I can't find my uke. Have you seen it, Leo? It's really important."

He squeezed his eyes tighter.

"It's going to be a terrible day," I whispered to Lily. "Why can't I lose things I don't like?" I peeked in the lunch bag on the table labeled LUCY MCGEE. "No potato chips! See? Dad put in zucchini sticks again! I hate zucchini. I wouldn't mind losing all the zucchini in the world!"

"Zuzu!" Lily said. She loves zucchini.

"I'm sorry. That was mean," I said. "I'm

sure zucchini tries hard to be a good vegetable, and I shouldn't have dissed it." I leaned in and whispered. "I'm just sad because I lost my uke. Don't tell Dad!"

Lily smiled, and then she reached out and patted me on the head with her gross, jelly-slimed hand. Yep, it was my lucky day.

Chapter Two

GUESS WHO'S NEWS?

"Lucy!" Phillip grabbed me as soon as I got to the blacktop, which is where we line up before school starts. Then he saw Resa and called her over. "Guys, guess who is coming to the Hamil Theater on Saturday?"

"The Queen of England?" Resa joked.

"Wrong," said Phillip.

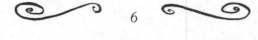

"Aliens?" Resa asked.

"No!" Phillip said. "Be serious! They're playing a concert. I heard about it on the radio. It's big news."

"I know!" Resa said. "Aliens playing ukuleles!"

"Okay," Phillip said with a smile. "I'd definitely want to see that." He pulled his uke out of his backpack. "Here's a hint." He started strumming a familiar tune. Resa pulled her uke out and started strumming with him. Seeing them play together made me feel even worse. I was ukeless.

Then Phillip started singing, "*After all these trips and falls, I'm gonna get up, gonna get up again.*"

"Get Up" was a Ben & Bree song. Ben & Bree are stars who sing and play ukulele all over the world. We watch their videos and try to play their songs in our Songwriting Club.

"Ben & Bree are coming?" I asked.

Phillip nodded and grinned and started singing their song again. That caught the attention of Scarlett, Victoria, and Mara, who ran over and started singing along. Everybody in our Songwriting Club loves Ben & Bree.

"Ben & Bree are doing a concert here on Saturday," Phillip told them. "We all have to ask our parents to get tickets."

Scarlett started jumping up and down, and then Victoria and then Mara. "I can't wait! I love them!" Scarlett said.

"It would be so fun if everybody in our Songwriting Club went together," Resa said. "Don't Ben & Bree give give away a free ukulele at the end of their shows?"

I couldn't believe my ears. "Did you just say they give away a ukulele?"

Phillip nodded. "They do it at every concert."

I grabbed Phillip's uke and sang, *"I have to go see Ben & Bree! I have to win a ukulele!"*

Phillip laughed. "The Hamil holds one thousand people, so we'd each have a one in one thousand chance of winning."

"I'm going to keep my fingers crossed until the show," Scarlett said.

I crossed my fingers, too.

"If we go, I hope one of us wins," Resa said. "We need a ladybug to land on us. My grandma says you'll have good luck if a ladybug lands on you."

I handed Phillip back his uke and looked up at the bright blue sky. Holding out my arms, I

called out, "Ladybug, ladybug, fly to me! Give me luck and then fly free!"

"I don't think any ladybugs heard you, Lucy," Scarlett said. "But look at that!"

A big black crow was heading in our direction . . . closer and closer. . . it was flying right over. . . oh no!

Plup.

Something landed on my head. My friends stared.

"What just happened?" I yelped, afraid to touch my hair.

They all answered at once.

"You got slimed."

"You got gooped."

"You got glopped."

"You got plooped."

Yup. Lucky me, Lucy McGee.

Chapter Three

MR. CHEEZZA, PLEASE

My poor hair. I felt sorry it belonged to me. If my hair was on Scarlett's head, a bird would probably drop a pretty flower on it instead of a load of you-know-what. Scarlett is one of those kids who has good luck all the time.

I needed some luck, so I kept my fingers crossed, which made washing my hair in the bathroom sink even harder. By the time I got the ploop out, math had started.

I wanted to sit by the window just in case a ladybug flew in, but Mrs. Brock wouldn't let me.

"Lucy, we're working on probability," my teacher said. "Have a seat and do the assignment!"

I looked at the paper in front of me.

PROBABILITY GAME

Imagine you are playing a game by spinning this wheel.

If you land on a prize, you win it.

Use fractions to calculate the following:

1. What is the probability that you will win a free boat?

2. What is the probability that you will win a free bicycle?

3. What is the probability that you will win nothing?

The probability of me, Lucy McGee, winning a free boat or a free bike was zero. I had bad, bad luck. If I played this game, I would land on *No Prize*. No Prize should be my middle name. Lucy No Prize McGee.

I wrote in my answers. The game wheel looked like a pizza, which made me think of Cheezza Pizza, which is where we went to dinner on Saturday night. Yum, I love pizza. My stomach started to growl. Wait a minute! I brought my uke to Cheezza Pizza! When it's somebody's birthday at Cheezza Pizza, everybody sings, and I wanted to whip out my uke and sing, but nobody had a birthday. I wanted to pretend it was Leo's birthday so we could sing, but my parents said that would be lying. Leo pretends he is an animal every day, and they never tell him he's lying. Little kids have it easy. But that wasn't the point. The point was, I must have left my uke at Cheezza Pizza! What if Mr. Cheezza was waiting to see if someone would call about the uke? What if he was about to throw it away or give it away? I had to call and find out!

I raised my hand.

Mrs. Brock gave me a look. "Does your question have to do with the assignment?"

I put my hand down.

Jeremy Bing raised his hand, and Mrs. Brock went over to his desk. She always helps Jeremy Bing.

Hmm . . . I had to figure out a way to call Cheezza Pizza. Then I saw it. There on Mrs. Brock's desk . . . her cell phone! Mrs. Brock uses her phone sometimes for quick facts. She talks into it, like, "How many miles is it from the Earth to the moon?" And then it answers or goes to a site with a diagram that she shows us.

Would it be terrible if I pushed one little button and sent a message to Cheezza Pizza? This was an emergency, after all. My brain said: *Don't do it!* My finger said: *Do it!*

Mrs. Brock's back was to me.

I took my paper up to her desk and set it on the done pile. Her phone was staring at me. *Don't do it,* my brain said again. My finger pushed the

button. The phone lit up. I
leaned over and whispered,
"Send a message to Cheezza
Pizza."

"Calling Cheezza Pizza," the voice said, and
the phone started beeping.

Everybody looked up.

"Cheezza Pizza here," said a man's voice on
the phone. "What would you like to order?"

Some kids started laughing, and Mrs. Brock
walked over. "Lucy! What are you doing with
my phone?"

"It sounds like she's trying to order pizza,"
Jeremy said.

I didn't want to lie, but I didn't want to admit
the truth either. See, the uke wasn't really mine.
We get to check out ukes like library books here
at Slido Creek Elementary School. If the school
found out that I lost their ukulele, I'd have to

pay for it. And I probably wouldn't get to be in the Songwriting Club anymore!

"I'm sorry, Mrs. Brock," I said.

She picked up my math paper. "Lucy, you didn't even follow directions. What happened to your brain today?"

"It got slimed by a bird," Scarlett said, and everybody started to laugh.

Ha ha. Not.

Chapter Four

THE LOSER BLUES

One of the things my dad says he loves the most about me is what he calls "the pep in my step." *Pep* means energy. I think *pep* comes from the word *pepper* because pepper spices up your food with energy.

Mondays and Wednesdays are usually my peppiest days. After school on Mondays, Phillip and Resa and I practice playing our ukuleles on the playground. On Wednesdays we have Songwriting Club in Ms. Adamson's room.

Today was a Monday and as soon as school was over, Phillip and Resa were ready. They grabbed their ukes from their cubbies, and the three of us started walking down the hall together. That's when Phillip noticed I didn't have mine.

"Where's your uke, Lucy?" Phillip asked.

I stopped. Should I confess? Sometimes when you're blue, it helps to tell a friend or two, I thought to myself. And then I thought, Hey, you know you're a songwriter if you make up rhymes when you're not even trying.

"I lost my uke," I said.

"That's bad." Phillip scrunched his face.

"Where did you lose it?" Resa asked.

"I don't know. That's the problem," I said. "I looked all over my house. The last place I remember having it was Cheezza Pizza."

"That's why you were calling them!" Resa said.

"Here." Phillip pulled a cell phone out of his backpack. "My mom said I'm supposed to use it only for emergencies. A lost uke is definitely an emergency."

"Thanks, Phillip."

They huddled around and crossed their fingers for me. I couldn't cross mine because I had to push the buttons. I called Cheezza Pizza, asked about the uke, and held my breath. The voice of Mr. Cheezza gave me the news. No luck.

Phillip put his phone back in his pack. "You'll find it before Wednesday," Phillip said. "So don't tell Ms. Adamson you lost it yet. Did you look in your car?"

"No," I said. "That's a great idea."

"Do you want to borrow my uke today?" Resa asked.

I smiled. My heart was sinking into a mud puddle of sadness, but at least my friends were giving me hope.

We had fun singing, and Resa and Phillip both took turns letting me play their ukes. As soon as our practice was over, I ran home and looked in our car.

Please . . . Please . . . Please . . .

Nothing.

I checked the garage and the backyard. And I double-checked the big stinky garbage can, just in case.

Please . . . Please . . . Please . . .

Big fat zero.

I was going to have to tell my parents soon. On Wednesday they'd want to know why I wasn't bringing my uke to school. They'd get mad. Then I'd have to tell Ms. Adamson. She'd get madder. My life was not looking good.

I sat on the front steps and made up a song. When you're feeling bad, sometimes you have to let it out. And if you're like me, Lucy McGee, it will probably come out in a rhyme.

I'm a loser. I got no luck.
When a bird flies by, I forget to duck.

Four-leaf clover? Just makes me sneeze.
Cough near me, I'll get a disease.

Come to my pity party, please, oh please.
Come to my pity party, please!

If it rains on my house, expect a flood.
At the end of my rainbow is a pot of mud.

Lucky ladybugs hide when I appear.
If I see a bee, it'll sting my rear.

Come to my pity party, please, oh please.
Come to my pity party, please!

Okay. That was fun.

When you're sad, write a song and you'll be glad.

Chapter Five

GOT GRIT?
DON'T QUIT!

There was only one thing left to do. I had to talk my parents into getting me a ticket so I could win that free uke.

When I walked in, my dad and Leo were on the couch reading a book.

"Come and join us, Lucy," my dad said. "Lily's upstairs taking a snooze."

Leo usually jumps on me like a puppy as soon as I get home. But he curled up like he did this morning.

"Hey, are you feeling like a turtle again, Leo?" I asked. He didn't answer, so I dove right in. "Dad!" I said in my peppy voice. "Did you hear the big news?"

"What news?" he asked.

I danced around the room. "Ben & Bree are coming to the Hamil Theater this Saturday! Going to a concert would put so much pep in my step, and I know you love that. Can I please go? Please? Please?"

My dad smiled. "I saw an ad for that in the

newspaper," he said. "I know you like them, but the tickets cost too much. Sorry, Lucy."

The pep in my step went *kerplop*.

I've heard that money is the roof of all evil. I'm not sure what that means. I just wish everything was free.

I stomped into the kitchen. Not a good beginning, but it wasn't over yet. My dad always said McGees have grit, which means we don't quit. I would show him!

On the kitchen table was the newspaper. There, on the second page, was an ad for the big Ben & Bree concert. Next to the ad was an article about all the reasons why adding vegetables to your diet makes you healthier. It was written by an expert.

That gave me an idea.

I grabbed my notebook and wrote my own article, and then I taped it into the newspaper. By the time I went back into the living room, Leo was asleep and my dad had his eyes closed.

"Dad," I whispered. "There's an interesting article in the newspaper. Can I read it to you?"

My dad opened his eyes. "Sure, Lucy."

I read my article, only I didn't say it was *my* article.

TOP THREE WAYS TO BE THE BEST PARENT

If you want to be the greatest dad or mom, here are three things that experts say you can do:

1.   Buy your child a ticket to see a wonderful music show. Music is good for children and good for the world. If your child asks you for a ticket, that's even better. Just think, you could have a kid

who wants money to buy junk food. Instead, you have a good kid who wants to hear her favorite act. So pat yourself on the back and buy that ticket!

2. Being the best parent means being cool. How do you get cool? The coolest parents take their kids to music shows. If you do this, everybody will think you're cool even though you wear clothes that make you look old and funny sometimes.

3. Be full of surprises! Let's say your daughter's birthday isn't for a while. Surprise her by getting her a birthday present right now. Wow! That would make you the best parent ever.

I closed the newspaper. "What do you think?"

"I read the paper today," my dad said. "I must have missed that article."

"I thought it had some good advice," I said.

He smiled. "Lucy, that was very creative. But I'm still not going to get you a ticket."

I stomped off to my room and sat on my pillow in my closet. If you know me, you know that I do some of my best thinking in my closet. And some of my best writing.

Dear Dad,

You're always telling me to "think before I leap," but I feel like you're leaping to NO without thinking at all. Have you thought about the terrible things that will happen if you DON'T get me a ticket to the Ben + Bree Show?

1.   If you don't, I will cry so much my face will be red and puffy and I will no longer be a cute daughter, and every time you look at my face, you will be sad and embarrassed.

2.   If you don't, you will feel guilty because many, many other parents are saying yes, and everyone will know you're cheap.

Please think about these things and let me know when you're ready to talk.

Your good daughter,

Lucy

I folded the letter in half. Usually Leo delivers my letters for me. He pretends he is an owl and grabs them in his beak. I missed Owl Leo. Turtle Leo isn't as useful. I gave my dad my letter, ran back into my closet, and made up a new song. It went like this:

Please, please, please, please, please,
please, please.

Please, please, please, please, please.

With sugar on top.

Chapter Six

MEMORIES OF BEES
AND A HUG FOR ME

"Knock, knock." My dad's voice came through my closet door.

"Who's there?" I asked.

"Dad," he said.

"The kind of dad who makes dreams come true?" I asked, crossing my fingers.

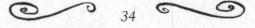

He opened the door, holding Lily in his arms. Lily had a sleepy after-nap look, and she was sucking on her pacifier.

"Lucy, come on out," my dad said. "Let's talk."

Thud. That was the sound of my heart falling down. "Let's talk" is not good news. Parents don't say "let's talk" before they give you what you want.

I crawled out of the closet, sat on my bed, and hugged my pillow. He pulled up my desk chair and sat in it with Lily. "Lucy, here's why I'm still saying no. First of all—"

"But—"

"Let me finish. First of all, threats don't work. You can cry all you want, and it's not going to make any difference. That doesn't make me a bad parent, and it doesn't mean I don't love you. Second, I don't care what other parents do. Third, no means no. So that means no more begging. Do you get it?"

I looked at the pillow in my lap.

"And don't ask Mom when she comes home," my dad said. "No from either of us means no. Do you remember what happened when you kept begging for a puppy?"

How could I forget? They told me that I had to stop begging, and I got mad at them and stomped outside in the backyard and plopped on the ground, except I landed on a bee! Ouch!

"Are we good?" my dad asked.

I didn't move.

My dad pulled away the pillow. "Lucy, say something. I can't have two turtles in the house."

Lily took her pacifier out of her mouth and pointed it at me and said, "No Tutta."

I felt a song coming on. I sang:

I'm sad and squashed like a poor, ugly bug.
What I need right now is an itty-bitty hug.

My dad smiled. Lily crawled out of my
dad's arms and gave me a hug. Her
little body was warm and smelled like
peanut butter and sleep.

When nothing is going your way and your
heart has fallen onto the floor with a thud, there's
one thing that can make you feel at least a little
lucky: a hug.

I hugged her back. She put her face really
close to mine and looked at me with big serious
eyes like she was trying to understand how I

felt. And then she took out her pacifier and tried to put it in my mouth.

My dad and I both laughed. "No thanks, Lily," I said. "But it's nice of you to want to share."

Chapter Seven

CRUNCH FOR LUNCH?

It took all my strength, but when my mom came home from work last night, I did not ask her for tickets. I knew that begging would send my dad exploding through the roof of all evil.

I think he appreciated me because guess what he put in my lunch this morning?

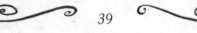

Potato chips!

I was still sad that I wasn't going to the concert. And I was still worried about the missing ukulele. But on the way to school, a thought popped into my head. Maybe, just maybe, one of the other kids would get tickets and invite me. There were ten people in our Songwriting Club. That meant I had a one-in-ten chance of getting a ticket.

Phillip was waiting for me by the fence. His back was to me, so I couldn't tell if he was happy or sad.

Please be happy. Please be happy. Please be happy.

I ran up, and he turned around. He looked like a sad puppy.

"No luck?" I guessed.

"Too expensive," Phillip said.

Resa came running up.

"Is your mom letting you go?" I asked her.

"She said yes," Resa said.

"What?" I started jumping up and down.

She rolled her eyes. "She said yes, I can go when I'm a teenager. What about you?"

I stopped jumping. "My dad said no."

We heard a squeal. Scarlett was running toward us.

"I got tickets!" she said.

Victoria and Mara heard her and ran over, too.

Scarlett danced around, and I started dancing, too. She said "tickets," not "ticket." This was good news!

"My mom said the show was very expensive, but she knew how much I wanted to go."

"How many tickets did you get?" I asked.

"Four," she said. "One for me. One for my mom. One for my sister, Brandy. And one extra—because my dad said he doesn't want to go. My mom said I can pick somebody from my class to go with me."

I dropped to my knees. "Please take me, Scarlett! Please. Please. Please."

"What about me?" Victoria asked.

"I'm the one who told everybody about the show," Phillip said.

Resa coughed. "You have to give it to me, Scarlett. I'm dying, and this is my last wish."

"Ha ha," Scarlett said.

"If I get picked and win the uke," I said, "I promise I'll share it with everybody."

"I don't care about the uke," Phillip said. "I just want to see them play."

"Everybody wants the ticket," Resa said. "This could get ugly."

Scarlett looked at all of us and smiled. It wasn't exactly a nice smile. It was more like the kind of smile a queen would give when she knows everybody wants to try on her crown. Then she said, "Giving away a ticket to one of you would be a very nice thing for me to do, so whoever really wants the ticket will probably want to do something very nice for me."

Victoria reached into her backpack and pulled out a glitter pen. "Here, Scarlett. I know you like these."

"Thank you, Victoria! I do like glitter pens."

Mara pulled off her bracelet. "Here, Scarlett. I know you like bracelets."

Scarlett put it on.

"Oh brother," Phillip said. "I can't win."

I checked my backpack. Besides homework, all I had was a dirty tissue, an empty candy wrapper, and my lunch. No way I was giving my potato chips to Scarlett.

Phillip tapped me. "Let's go see if anybody else from the Songwriting Club got tickets."

"I'm coming," Resa said.

The three of us ran over to where the fifth graders were lining up. Pablo, Natalie, and Saki all said no luck. We found Riley and asked him. His parents had said no way.

"This is horrible," Phillip said. "We have to

bribe Scarlett. But she probably won't pick us anyway."

He and Resa started looking through their backpacks to see what they could give Scarlett. I looked at my lunch again.

The bell rang for school to start. As we were walking in, I said, "Scarlett, I have something for you."

And then I gave her my potato chips. My salty, crunchy, lovely potato chips.

"A crunch for your lunch," I said.

Not even the rhyme cheered me up.

Chapter Eight

THE PRICE OF BEING NICE

On the way to the classroom, Mara carried Scarlett's backpack for her.

"I'm thirsty," Scarlett said, and when she stopped for a drink, Victoria turned on the drinking fountain.

As soon as we got to the classroom, Phillip rolled his eyes and said, "I can't believe I'm doing this." Then he handed his brand-new pencil to Scarlett. Phillip loves new pencils.

"If you can't beat them, join them," Resa said. And then she added, "Let me sharpen that for you, Scarlett," and she grabbed the pencil and ran over to the sharpener.

Scarlett sat at her desk and said, "I think I have a little dirt on my shoe."

Mara ran to the tissue box, and Victoria raced to the paper towel holder. And then they both polished Scarlett's pretty pink shoes.

"This is fun," Scarlett said. "You know what? I have cage cleaning duty this week, and I hate that."

"I'll do it for you!" I ran over to Mr. Chomper's cage. Mr. Chomper is the hamster who lives in our classroom. When Mrs. Brock first got him, Resa brought in a dollhouse toilet to put in his cage, but Mr. Chomper still goes wherever he wants to go. We all like Mr. Chomper, but nobody likes cleaning his cage.

"Lucy," Mrs. Brock said. "Isn't it Scarlett's job this week?"

"Yes," I said. "But I'm doing it. It's just something nice I want to do for Scarlett." I looked back at Scarlett and smiled.

After the morning routine, Mrs. Brock told us to get out our math books.

"I forgot mine," Scarlett whispered.

When one of us forgets a book, Mrs. Brock allows us to borrow one of hers from the shelf. So Victoria, Mara, Resa, Phillip, and I jumped up and ran to get a book for Scarlett,

and . . . *BAM!* We all crashed into each other. Victoria and Mara knocked heads. Phillip fell down. And I tripped over Resa and landed in Jeremy Bing's lap!

"What is going on?" Mrs. Brock exclaimed.

I jumped up.

Jeremy was speechless.

The other kids in our class started laughing.

"Sorry, Mrs. Brock," Victoria said quickly. "I just wanted to get a book for Scarlett."

"My friends were all just trying to be nice to me," Scarlett said.

Mrs. Brock gave us that look. "I'm sure Scarlett is able to get her own book. Everybody sit down and get to work."

I was kind of happy about getting to work. Being nice to Scarlett was way harder than math. Then came lunch, which was terrible because I had to watch Scarlett crunch every single one of my crispy-wispy potato chips.

Finally, recess came. Phillip, Resa, and I wanted to play a game called Steam Run. But Victoria and Mara kept doing nice things for Scarlett, and it was driving us crazy. We wanted to have recess, but we didn't want to lose our chance at getting picked by Scarlett.

"Scarlett," Phillip said, "Please pick somebody so we can all get on with our lives."

Scarlett thought for a minute. Then her eyes lit up. "Let's have a contest. Whoever wins gets my extra ticket."

"What's the contest about?" Victoria said.

"Handstands!" Resa said, and she dove into a handstand. She can walk on her hands for ten seconds.

"Juggling!" Phillip said. He picked up three pinecones and started to juggle.

Oh no! I didn't have a trick. I was starting to panic when Scarlett said something *sweeeeet*.

"The prize is a music ticket, so the contest should be about music," she said. "I'll give everybody one minute to write a song. Whoever's song is the best wins."

I started jumping up and down. "I love writing songs!"

"One minute isn't enough time to write a whole song," Victoria said.

"Write a short song," Scarlett said. "I'll count backwards from sixty to one. Go!"

"Not fair!" Resa said. "Give us time to think."

"Sixty . . . Fifty-nine . . . " Scarlett counted.

"Fifty-eight . . . "

I needed peace and quiet. I ran behind a tree.
Think. Think. Think.

Chapter Nine

MY CRAZY BRAIN
STRIKES AGAIN

"Can the song be about anything?" I heard Mara ask.

"Yes," Scarlett said.

As Scarlett continued counting down, my thoughts started arguing with each other. It was like I had two brains in my head, and they were fighting.

You have to win this contest. Write a song now, Lucy!

—*Be quiet! I'm trying to think of an idea!*

How about a song about school?

—*Boring!*

A song about Mr. Chomper?

—*Worse.*

How about a song about Scarlett counting down?

—*Be serious! This is your big chance. You come up with an idea!*

—*Okay, how about a song about dirt? Oh. Lovely.*

—*You're wasting time, Lucy! Just pick an idea and go with it.*

I would if you would be quiet.

—*Me? You're the one making all the noise.*

"Time's up!" Scarlett said.

Sixty seconds had flown by. I was doomed.

Scarlett sat on the picnic table like it was a throne and held out her arms and said, "Let the songs begin! Victoria, you can start."

Victoria got a look on her face that made me think she'd had trouble writing her song, too. "I wanted to make a longer song," she said. "But a fly kept bugging me, and I couldn't concentrate." And then she sang:

Scarlett is my best friend.
She's pretty and she isn't twitty.
Scarlett. Scarlett. Scarlett.
Scarlett. Scarlett. Scarlett.

Scarlett clapped. "That was beautiful. Who's next?"

Mara sang:

Everyone loves Scarlett.
She's a girl who is so nice.
Everyone loves Scarlett.
Even little mice.

"Aw," Scarlett said. "That's cute. Thanks, Mara."

I should have written a song about Scarlett. I didn't like their songs, but Scarlett did. Victoria and Mara were smart.

"Who's next?" Scarlett asked.

Resa stood up. "I'll go next. I didn't write about you, Scarlett. I wrote about a bird."

Scarlett frowned.

"You said it could be about anything," Resa said. "I saw a bird, and it reminded me of that bird going to the bathroom on Lucy's head."

"This is going to be good," Phillip said.

"I don't think I want to be reminded," I said.

Resa wants to be a stand-up comedian when she grows up, and she is good at making us laugh, so we knew this would be funny. She put her arms out as if they were wings and sang.

> *I am a bird; I fly through the air.*
> *I gobble bugs here and there.*
> *When I'm in the sky, you should beware.*
> *I might ploop my goop on your hair.*

Everybody laughed.

"Good song, Resa," Phillip said.

"Funny and true," I said.

"Thank you!" Resa said.

That was hard to beat.

Phillip stood up. He sang:

My name is Phillip Lee.
You should pick me.
'Cause I taught you all to play the ukulele.
I got fingers like lightning.
I sing amazingly.
I'm the biggest, baddest fan of Ben &
Bree.

Resa and I clapped.
Phillip bowed.
"Your turn, Lucy,"
Scarlett said.
My two brains started
arguing again.

Lucy, make up a song
right now. It has to be great.
—Be quiet! I'm trying to think.

Then I started singing.

*I've got two brains in my mixed-up
head.*
They don't get along. They fight instead.
One says yes and the other says no.
One says fast and the other says slow.
One hates my guts and the other thinks
I'm fine.
*I want to trade them in for a brand-new
mind.*

 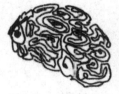

Everybody clapped. I did it! I did it!
Phillip nodded at me. "Hate to admit it, but
that was good."

We all looked at Scarlett. The big moment arrived. She bit a nail and got a worried look on her face. "I didn't think of this before," she said. "But if I pick one of you, then the rest of you will be mad at me."

We were all quiet. It was kind of true. I wouldn't want to be in her shoes, even though they were polished!

A few seconds passed. I crossed my fingers so tight I was afraid they'd never come apart.

Finally, she shook her head. "I can't do it. Forget the contest."

Phillip plopped down on the ground. "Oh brother!"

The bell rang. Recess was over.

"You have to pick somebody!" Victoria said.

"Do something fair like draw straws or roll a dice or pick a card to win," Resa said.

"Something that doesn't make us

all your servants," Phillip
said as he got up from the
ground.

"Something that gives everybody the same
chance," I said.

"Okay," Scarlett said. "I'll think about it and
come up with a new plan tomorrow."

"Uh-oh. Don't look up," Resa said.

We all looked up. A bird was flying right
toward us.

"Aaaaaaah!" we all screamed, and ran in.

Chapter Ten

WHY NOT TRY?

Here's a great question: Why aren't four-leaf clovers red? I wish they were red, because then they'd be easier for me to find, and I'd have better luck. After school, I looked in my front and backyard for a lucky clover. All I found were grass and ants.

If Scarlett made us pick numbers or draw cards

tomorrow, I was definitely going to lose. I had to do something.

An idea popped into my brain. I could go to Scarlett's house and convince her that she should pick me. It would be a lot easier to do it if it was just her and me talking.

I ran inside. Lily saw me and came running over to hug my knees—except it was a funny kind of shuffle because she was wearing my dad's shoes. She had his hat on, too.

"Hi, Lily!" I said.

"Dess," she said, which is her word for dress up. She dragged me into the living room. The floor was covered with costumes and my dad was sitting in the middle with a tutu on his head.

"Very cute, Dad," I said.

"Thanks," he said, catching Lily who dove into his lap.

Leo turned into a turtle and crawled behind my dad. It was getting to be all turtle all the time with that kid.

"Can I walk over to Scarlett's and ask her something?" I asked. "It won't take long."

"Sure," he said. "But make it short, Lucy. I need a break so I can get dinner going."

"Do we have any fancy cookies?" I asked.

"Why?" he asked.

"Scarlett loves them."

He gave me a look. "What's going on, Lucy?"

I sighed. "Scarlett has an extra ticket to the Ben & Bree show, and I want her to pick me. So why not bring her over a few cookies?"

My dad sighed. "You can't bribe friends, Lucy."

"I can try," I said.

He gave me his serious look. "Lucy, you can go to Scarlett's, but no cookies."

"Fine," I said. "I'll use my words to convince her."

"No begging!" he said.

"But—"

He shook his head. "Begging is annoying."

"You know, Dad," I said. "If grown-ups thought kids were cute when we beg, our lives would be a lot easier."

He laughed. "Well, that was pretty cute."

"Can I have a ticket now, please?"

"Nope."

It was my turn to sigh. "You tell me not to be a quitter, but then you tell me to quit begging."

He smiled. "Yep. The rules of life are complicated, but I think you know in your heart of hearts what's right."

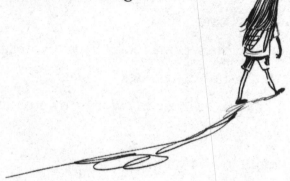

I promised not to be annoying, and I grabbed my backpack and walked to Scarlett's. I could see the front of her house and the driveway of the school from my house, which is why I got to walk there on my own. As I walked, I practiced what I was going to say to her. By the time I reached her house, I was ready!

Chapter Eleven

ME, AND A CAT, AND
. . . WHO'S THAT?

I knocked on Scarlett's door. No
answer. I stepped over to the front
window and peered in.

Her living room was dark. *WHOOSH!* Out of
nowhere a face came at me in the window. Spooked, I
jumped back and—*WHOA!*—tripped over a bush.

CRASH! I fell right on my rear.

There, perched in the window and hissing at me was Princess Coconut, Scarlett's cat.

To say that Princess Coconut doesn't like me is not strong enough. She hates me. I don't know why.

I picked myself up and brushed off the dirt. Then I went into the backyard to see if Scarlett was in the shed, which Scarlett calls her Craft Cottage. Empty. No car in the driveway, either.

Just my luck. Nobody home.

I couldn't go home without doing something, so I sat on her patio, pulled a pencil and paper out of my backpack, and wrote her a letter.

Dear Scarlett,

You are my best friend because
you're so sweet and smart and all I
think about is how much I want to be like you.

My heart knew that wasn't true. I tried
again.

Hi Scarlett,

　　You have a ticket. I want a ticket. Let's work
out a trade. If you give me that ticket, I'll give
you whatever of mine that you want. You wouldn't
want my clothes or shoes because yours are way
nicer than mine. I don't have any money. So that's
out. You always say you hate having a little sister,
so what about Leo? I couldn't give him to you
forever because we would miss him, but you could
have him for a day. For example, on a day when he
is being a turtle, which is cute.

Okay. My heart knew that last part was a lie.
Leo is cute when he's being a wolf or an owl or
a duck or a puppy or a pig or a bush baby or a
wallaby, but he isn't fun when he's being a turtle.

As I finished, I could feel eyes on me. I looked up, and there in the window was Princess Coconut again. She was looking at me out the back window as if she wanted to pounce on my head.

Just then a noise came from the side of the house. Someone was coming. Since no car had pulled up, it couldn't be Scarlett. A scary thought popped into my head. What if it was a robber?

I jumped up and ran behind the Craft Cottage.

It was strange. . . . It sounded like something was rolling on the ground. . . . It was probably a robber rolling a huge suitcase along to put stuff in. If I jumped out, maybe I would save the day, and Scarlett's parents would give me a whole bunch of tickets. Or maybe the bad guy would stuff me in the suitcase!

I was still trying to decide when I heard another sound. I think the robber heard it, too, because the sound of the rolling stopped.

A new set of footsteps were coming from the other side of the house. Another robber! Scarlett's parents were very rich. Bad guys were probably always watching their house to see when no one was home. I never should have come! I was probably going to get kidnapped, and I'd never see my parents or Leo or Lily or my friends again! They would miss me, and I would miss them. Poor Leo would be so sad, he would probably stay in his turtle shell forever.

Chapter Twelve

BAD GUYS' SURPRISE

Since there were now two robbers, one that I heard on the right side of the house and one on the left, I decided the safest thing was to stay hidden behind the cottage. I took a step back, and—*CRASH!*—I tripped over a little tree stump. *BLAM!* On my rear a second time!

A scary silence followed.

The robbers knew I was back there, so I decided to make a run for it. I ran out, screaming, and the bad guys started screaming, too. Except they weren't bad guys. One was Phillip holding his bike, and the other was Resa.

We stopped screaming and stared at each other.

"What are you doing here, Lucy?" Phillip asked.

"What are you doing here, Phillip?" I asked.

"What are you both doing here?" Resa asked. "You guys almost gave me a heart attack."

"This is embarrassing," Phillip said. "We all know why we're here. We're all trying to get that ticket."

"It's life or death for me," I said. "I need to win that ukulele."

"You still haven't found yours?"

I shook my head.

"What did your parents say?" Phillip asked.

"I haven't even told them," I said.

"Yikes," Resa said.

Phillip looked at Resa. "Maybe we could help Lucy buy a new one."

Resa reached in her pocket. "Yeah, I'm rich. I've got seven cents."

I laughed.

"We could do something to earn the money," Phillip said. "You know . . . like a lemonade stand. When I was six, I made ten bucks doing that, and the lemonade was terrible."

"If we sold something more valuable than lemonade, we could earn more money," Resa said.

"That's so nice," I said. "But—"

"I've got it!" Phillip said. "Come on!"

He rolled his bike back out of the driveway, and the three of us walked to the corner. He parked

his bike and took his uke out of his backpack.
"Take off your hat, Resa," he said. "And put it on
the ground. We're going to sing, and people are
going to throw money into the hat!"

"You're insane, Phillip," Resa
said.

"Let's do it!" I said.

Resa put her seven cents
into the hat so people
would get the idea. Phillip had
a quarter, which he added.

"What should we sing?"
Phillip asked.

I taught them my pity party song, and we sang it.

I'm a loser. I got no luck.
When a bird flies by, I forget to duck.

Four-leaf clover? Just makes me sneeze.
Cough near me, I'll get a disease.

Come to my pity party, please, oh please.
Come to my pity party, please.

Two cars went by.

We made up some new verses.

An old guy walking his dog passed us. The dog stopped and sniffed at the hat. We kept singing. The guy reached into his pocket! And then he pulled out a tissue and blew his nose. "Catchy song," he said, and kept walking.

"At least he didn't leave us his snot rag," Resa whispered.

We kept singing.

When I cross my fingers, all I get is an ache.
If I drop something fancy, it's gonna break.

Come to my pity party, please, oh please.
Come to my pity party, please.

Two middle school kids were coming on bikes. Uh-oh. They were probably going to tease us. They were probably going to say something really mean. They slowed down.

"Just keep singing," Phillip whispered.

My genie in a bottle? Got shipped to France.
I get no prize when the game is chance.

Come to my pity party, please, oh please.
Come to my pity party, please.

They stopped and listened to us. At the end of our song, there was silence. And then one said, "That was funny."

The other nodded. "Yeah. Not bad."

"Thanks!" Phillip said.

"Feel free to tip us," Resa said.

I thought they would laugh.

"We don't have any money," the first one said. "But that's cool."

They rode off.

Phillip looked at me. "Did he just say we were cool?"

We didn't make money, but it still felt great.

We played a few more songs. A woman passing by with her kids stopped and gave her kids each a quarter to put in the hat.

"Thanks!" we called out.

And then one of her kids ran back and threw something else in the hat.

We all looked.

A gumball.

"That's kind of gross," Resa said. "And kind of sweet at the same time."

Phillip dumped the change and the gumball into my hand. "It's all yours, Lucy!"

I got a big feeling inside me. I mean, I know it wasn't much, but it made me feel so good. I felt like my heart was the hat, and my friends just poured a thousand dollars into it. You don't need money to feel rich. All you need are good friends.

Chapter Thirteen

WILL IT BE ME?

On Wednesday a little bit of luck came my way. Before school, Ms. Adamson sent a message to parents that she had to cancel Songwriting Club because she had to leave school early. *Whew!* That meant I had a little more time to find my uke.

I was excited to go to school because Scarlett was

going to pick one of us fair and square, and it could be me.

Because it was raining, we went inside right away instead of lining up on the playground. So, as soon as we put our backpacks in our cubbies, we all huddled around Scarlett's cubby.

"I've written your names down on these pieces of paper," Scarlett said, showing us five little folded notes. "I'll mix them up and pick one."

"Let's do it now," Phillip said. "Before Mrs. Brock starts the morning routine."

We crouched down in a circle.

Everybody crossed their fingers.

"Scarlett, even though they all look alike, you should close your eyes to make sure it's fair," Mara said.

Scarlett closed her eyes and shook the five little pieces of folded paper in her cupped hands and then tossed them onto the floor like dice.

I chanted in my head: *Let it be me, Lucy McGee. Let it be me, Lucy McGee. Let it be me, Lucy McGee.*

Scarlett picked up a piece of paper and unfolded it. "Victoria!" Scarlett read.

Victoria started jumping up and down. "I'm so excited. I can't believe it!"

Mara slumped.

"Sorry, Mara," Scarlett said. "It's not my fault. It was luck."

Scarlett swept up all the little pieces of paper and put them in the trash can.

Poof! Just like that, my dream of going to the concert and winning that ukulele was gone.

"All right, boys and girls," Mrs. Brock called out. "Let's get this day going."

Victoria and Scarlett went to their desks.

Phillip's forehead wrinkled. "Don't you guys think it was a little suspicious that Victoria won?" he whispered.

"Scarlett had her eyes closed when she picked, Phillip," Resa said. "I watched her."

"But what if . . . ?" Phillip looked over at the trash can.

Mrs. Brock called out. "Phillip, Resa, and Lucy, take your seats." She turned on *The Morning Mix*, which is the television news show the fifth graders put on every morning.

As we sat down, Phillip whispered, "We have to look at those papers!"

I glanced around the room. There had to be something to throw away. On the floor by Jeremy Bing's desk was a crumpled tissue. I didn't really want to touch Jeremy Bing's nose drippings, but this was important.

I walked over and picked up the tissue.

"What are you doing?"
Jeremy whispered.

"Just trying to keep our classroom clean," I said, and walked over to the trash can. Scarlett gave me a funny look.

The can was empty except for the Scarlett's five folded pieces of paper sitting on the bottom. I bent down, put the tissue in the can, and picked up the pieces of paper. I had them in my hand when I heard Phillip say, "Watch out!"

I looked up, and Scarlett bumped into my arm. The papers went flying.

"Sorry, Lucy," Scarlett said. "I didn't mean to bump into you." But she wasn't sorry. She raced to get the piece of paper that was closest to her. I picked up another. Phillip and Resa ran up and dove for the other pieces.

"What is going on?" Mrs. Brock asked.

I opened my paper. In Scarlett's handwriting was the name Victoria.

Phillip opened up the two he had in his hand, and Resa opened up the one in her hand. They read the names on the papers at the same time: "Victoria."

There were four Victorias!

"Show us yours, Scarlett," Phillip said.

86

Scarlett put her paper in her pocket. "I don't know what you're talking about."

"I bet it says Victoria," I said.

Phillip nodded. "You made sure there was a five in five chance of Victoria being chosen."

"I thought we were friends," Mara said sadly.

"Class," Mrs. Brock said, "what is going on?"

"A major crime has been committed," Phillip said.

Scarlett rolled her eyes. "I didn't commit a crime, Mrs. Brock. I just wrote Victoria's name five times by accident."

"Accident?" Resa laughed.

"Well, I suggest you work all that out after school," Mrs. Brock said. "In case you haven't noticed, we're in the middle of *The Morning Mix*."

It was over.

As we walked back to our seats, Phillip whispered, "My dream has been crumpled."

Resa nodded. "My dream has been crumpled and thrown into the trash."

I plopped into my seat. My dream? Crumpled and thrown into a trash can full of bird ploop.

Chapter Fourteen

UPS AND DOWNS
ALL AROUND

The day crawled by, and then after lunch something unexpected happened—all because Phillip had to go to the bathroom during science!

We had science the last period of the day, and when Phillip came back from the bathroom, I knew right away that something had happened.

His eyes were huge, but we were supposed to be working quietly on our projects. So he wrote a note. Resa was closest to him, so he passed it to her first. It had to be something good, because as she read it, she started smiling. Then she passed it to me.

I ran into Ms. Adamson as she was walking out the door. She said Ben & Bree just tweeted a special giveaway. Four last-minute tickets to Ben & Bree! To enter the giveaway, you post a video of yourself singing "Get Up" with a special hashtag. The deadline is tomorrow at midnight. They'll pick one video at random and give whoever made it four tickets to Saturday's show. Ms. Adamson asked me to tell everybody in the Songwriting Club because everybody is going to want to enter. I'm so excited!

I looked at Phillip and Resa. Their eyeballs were popping out. Mine probably were too, but I couldn't see them. We know all the Ben & Bree songs by heart. We could make a video. We could win. I wanted to get up and start dancing around the room, but I had to pretend like nothing was going on.

Just then Scarlett walked by my desk and snatched the note out of my hands. Before I could stop her, Scarlett took it to her desk and read it. Then she sent a note back to me.

This is so fun! I'm entering. My video is
going to be excellent because my mom has a
real video camera, not just a cell phone. I am
going to tell Victoria, but that's it. Don't tell
anybody else in the club or anybody period. The
more people who enter, the harder it will be to
win. If I win, I'll have four extra free tickets
and I'll give them to whoever in the whole
school is nicest to me—including you and Phillip
and Resa. So, you sort of have two chances.
You should be happy about that. —Scarlett

I shared the note with Phillip and Resa, and
then as soon as school got out, the three of us
had a meeting.

"Scarlett makes me mad," I said. "She's going
to win the tickets. I just know it."

"And then we'll have to polish her shoes
and do her chores, and she'll still probably give

the tickets to somebody else," Resa said.

"We should give up," I said.

"Guys!" Phillip said. "We can't give up. It's going to be a random pick. It doesn't matter if she has a fancy camera."

"But what if it isn't random?" I asked.

Resa jumped in. "I think if the video Ben & Bree picked at random was bad, they'd keep picking until they got a good one. If we're going to do this, we should make a really good one."

"Okay, then, let's make a great one," Phillip said. "Come on. We can do this. Go home and get permission to stay after school tomorrow. Practice as much as you can tonight! Tomorrow we'll bring our ukes, and we'll bring our best, most positive attitudes, and we'll make the most fantastic video ever!"

When Phillip gives a pep talk, he really gets into it.

"One for all, all for one!" Resa said, and put her fist in the middle for us to bump. We did a triple bump, and then we all turned to go.

I was so happy, but then I stopped.

"Wait," I said. "What about Scarlett's idea?"

I didn't even have to say what I meant. Were we going to do the right thing and tell everybody else in the club about the giveaway so they could enter, too, or were we going to take Scarlett's suggestion and keep it a secret?

We got quiet.

"If we don't tell them, and they find out, they'll hate us," Resa said. "I'd hate us."

Phillip chewed on his thumbnail. "This is what I call a conundrum. I want to keep it a secret, but I don't want to be selfish."

"Maybe we should just tell them," I said. "We'll feel better."

Phillip nodded. "I can get my mom to call everybody as soon as I get home," Phillip said. "She has a list of all the phone numbers of parents in school."

Resa shrugged. "Too bad they don't give free tickets to people for deciding to do the right thing. We'd have a better chance at winning those."

We did a triple fist bump again.

Now I was all the way happy.

Chapter Fifteen

BUSH BABIES
IN THE
DEEP BLUE
SEA

I couldn't wait to get home. I was going to tell my dad all about the exciting new contest, and then I was going to practice singing and playing so I'd be ready for tomorrow. Then I remembered the horrible truth—I didn't have a uke, and I hadn't told my parents it was lost! They were going to be so mad.

When I got home, my dad's famous tofu taco pie was baking, and he was playing on the kitchen floor with some bush babies. Not real bush babies. Just Lily and Leo. They were playing Bush Babies in a Boat. That's a game where you sit in a laundry basket in the middle of the floor and let your dad push you around, and you pretend you're a bush baby sailing in the deep blue sea. I loved it when I was little. Leo hopped out, but instead of running over and begging me to play, he gave me a funny look and ran out of the room.

"What's wrong with him?" I asked.

"I don't know," my dad said. "He was having fun sailing through a storm in the boat. Right, Lily?"

"Bo!" Lily said. "Bo!"

"What's wrong with you, Lucy?" my dad asked. "You're wearing your worried face."

Saying the truth out loud is really hard when the truth makes you look bad. So I didn't say anything.

"Bo!" Lily said. She tumbled out of the laundry basket and pushed it to me. "Lulu go bo!"

"She wants to give you a boat ride," my dad said.

Lily looked up at me and smiled with her big brown eyes.

"No thanks," I said.

She hugged me around the knees and tried to lift me up as if she could actually put me in! My dad laughed.

"Okay, bush baby," I said and climbed in. Even though I was squashed, I gave Lily a smile and said, "Wow. Nice boat!"

She was so happy. She danced around the boat like a baby dolphin, and then she stopped, put her face right up to mine, and blew out a big breath.

My dad laughed again. "Aye, captain," he said to me. "Looks like a balmy breeze is fillin' yer sails!"

"She must have gotten to taste your taco sauce before you put the pie in the oven because I can smell it on her breath," I said.

Lily grinned.

My dad started pushing me around the kitchen floor, and Lily kept dancing around me and blowing on my face.

"Shiver me timbers!" he said. "This vessel weighs a ton! Ye can't be a bush baby! Ye must be an elephant!"

Lily laughed. As my dad turned me around, I got a glimpse of Leo peeking in at us through the doorway. He saw me and then ran upstairs.

"What ho! A storm is brewin'!" my dad said.

This used to be my favorite part. Lily knew what to do. She grabbed a wooden spoon and started banging on a pot.

"Thunder and lightning!" my dad said as he started rocking the laundry basket back and forth. "The waves are a-comin'!"

I laughed and held on to the sides of the basket as my dad tried to tip me over, and

Lily did her lightning bolt dance. And then my dad gave a final roar and tumbled me out on the floor. "Elephant overboard!"

Lily jumped on me to save me, and my dad started tickling us both.

I was laughing and then something funny happened, and I sort of started to cry.

My dad dropped the pirate voice. "What's wrong, Lucy?"

Lily could tell it was serious. She crawled into my dad's lap and got quiet.

All the worries inside me wanted to tumble

out. "I lost my uke, and I've looked everywhere. And—"

"You lost your uke? When?"

"Monday. I've been worried about it all week."

"Why didn't you tell us?" he asked.

"I knew you and Mom would be mad at me for losing it," I said. "There'd be yelling and stomping and some kind of really big punishment because I was so bad. And now I want to enter a video contest to get tickets to the Ben & Bree show, but you probably won't let me."

My dad sighed. "Lucy. If you had told us right away, we'd have tried to help you find it," he said. "Could you have left it at school?"

"No," I said.

"Okay, before we jump to conclusions, let's get Leo and do a family search. Top to bottom," he said. "Come on! Let's go upstairs and try to find Lucy's ukulele!"

You know how a lighthouse is supposed to shine a little light from the shore so a boat can see where to go in a storm? Sometimes, my dad is a lighthouse for me.

Maybe an elephant, two bush babies, and a lighthouse could find that ukulele after all!

Chapter Sixteen

WHERE, OH WHERE?
IS MY UKE THERE?

"Leo!" my dad called out as we walked up the stairs.
"Calling all bush babies! Emergency search party!"

No answer. His bed was suspiciously lumpy. Even
Lily could tell he was hiding. She ran right over, climbed
up on his bed and started pounding on the lumps.

"Ouch!" Leo said, and threw off his blanket.

"Lucy lost her uke and we're going to help her find it," my dad said.

Leo got a guilty look on his face.

"Leo?" my dad asked. "Do you know where Lucy's uke is?"

He crawled back under his blanket.

"Leo!" I said and pulled it away again. "If you took my uke, you have to say so right now!"

He flipped over and pulled his pillow over his head.

"Tutta!" Lily said.

"This is not time to be a turtle, Leo," my dad said.

While my dad tried to get Leo out of his shell, I searched through his room. I looked in his closet and in his toy chest. Nothing.

"If you're too scared to talk, Leo, you must have done something really bad!" I said. "This is why you've been weird all week!"

Leo started to cry.

I dove under the bed and . . .

"My ukulele!" I yelled, and pulled it out.

And then I saw . . . one of the strings was hanging loose.

"I broke it!" Leo sobbed. "I wanted to play it. And you said no. So I took it. And I turned those things at the top, and I broke it."

"It was bad enough that you broke it," I yelled, "but not telling about it was even worse!"

"Lucy," my dad said, "let me see the uke and let me talk to Leo."

"You better punish him!" I said. "Because that was the baddest ever!"

Leo howled as I marched out.

I stomped down the stairs and stomped around the kitchen. All those days I was worrying! All because of Leo! I went to the

backyard and stomped around more. Then my feet hurt, so I sat in the tree swing.

After a while my dad came out with my ukulele in one hand and Lily on his hip.

"I looked online," he said. "A loose string is pretty easy to fix. See what you think." He handed it to me, and I strummed it.

"Sounds good," he said. "Right?"

It did. I was relieved but my heart still felt tight. "Leo made three huge mistakes. He took my uke. He turned the pegs at the top. And then he hid it."

"Yep," my dad said. "He knows he made a mistake and wants to apologize. He thinks you hate him. I bet you can cheer him up."

"Cheer him up?" I asked. "Why should I do that? He should be cheering *me* up."

He gave me a look. "Lucy, you were so happy that I didn't stomp and yell when you told me you couldn't find your uke. But what did you do when Leo finally confessed his mistake?"

My face got hot. It was confusing. My dad always tells me it's good to let my feelings out.

"I was so mad, I couldn't control myself," I said.

"Are you mad now?" he asked.

"Yeah," I said. "Sort of."

A second passed.

"Are you mad now?" he asked.

"Dad!"

"What about now?" He smiled. "You have a choice, Lucy. You can stay mad. Or you can have a big heart and come in and accept Leo's apology."

I took a breath and hopped off the swing. "Leo is lucky. I have a big heart."

My brother was sitting on the kitchen floor when we walked in. He looked like a mess. His eyes and cheeks were wet, and his nose was running. As soon as he saw me, he burst into tears again. "I'm sorry, Lucy. I promise to never steal your uke again."

That's when the rest of my mad melted away. I set my uke down on the kitchen table, and then I pulled the laundry basket over to where he was sitting. "Thanks, Leo," I said. "I'm sorry I yelled. Now, hop in!"

My dad set Lily on the floor, and she squealed and ran over.

Oh, a storm was a-coming, but now
we've got a breeze
   To sail our little ship across the deep
blue sea.
   Just a dad, two bush babies, a uke, and
me,
   Your famous singing captain, Lucy
McGee.

Chapter Seventeen

QUIET ON THE SET

"You found your uke!" Phillip exclaimed when I showed up the next day.

"My brother kidnapped it," I said, "but I got it back."

"Saki, Natalie, Pablo, and Riley are making a video together after school," Resa said. "And Mara said she's making one with her cousin."

"Let's just make ours good," Phillip said. "And let the best video win."

We pulled out our ukes and started practicing. Just then Scarlett and Victoria showed up with matching outfits. "We're going to make our video at my house after school," Scarlett said. "Isn't this fun?"

"Ignore her," Phillip whispered.

We wanted to practice more, but the whistle blew for us to go in.

"Good morning," Mrs. Brock said when we all walked in the classroom. "Step out of the way, please, so Mr. Tapper can get by. He had to put in a new lightbulb."

Mr. Tapper, the custodian, was climbing down from a ladder with an old lightbulb in his hand.

"It's not exactly a *good* morning, Mrs. Brock," Phillip said. "It's more like a *thumbnail-chewing* morning."

"A lot of us are entering a giveaway contest," I explained. "And we're going to make our videos after school. And then we won't find out until tomorrow who won."

"The Ben & Bree giveaway?" Mr. Tapper asked. "I just heard about that. I think I'm going to enter, too."

Our mouths dropped open.

He laughed and started singing "Get Up."

"Oh no," Resa said. "More competition for us."

Phillip nodded. "Yeah, but that's kind of cool, Mr. Tapper." He and Mr. Tapper fist-bumped.

"Victoria and I are going to enter, too, Mrs. Brock," Scarlett said.

"I'm entering, too," Mara said.

"Great!" Mrs. Brock rolled her eyes. "I bet we'll have problems focusing today."

"Don't worry. I won't have a hard time focusing," Scarlett said. "I don't care if I win or lose. It'll just be fun to enter."

Easy for her to say. She already had tickets!

At recess, we split into our groups and practiced. Scarlett and Victoria practiced on the blacktop. Saki, Natalie, Pablo, and Riley practiced by the fence. Phillip, Resa, and I practiced by the playground. Mara's cousin doesn't go to our school, so Mara didn't practice. She joined a four-square team. It was kind of strange for us to be doing different things, but it also made sense for us to be entering in groups. Whoever won would only get four tickets.

Then Scarlett called everybody in the Songwriting Club over to the picnic table for a meeting.

"If I win," Scarlett said, "I'll have four tickets to give away. So if you want one, you can fill out this form. I made them during math." She gave us each a piece of paper.

IN CASE SCARLETT WINS FOUR EXTRA TICKETS

Name:

Age:

Phone Number:

What Will You Do for Scarlett If She Gives You a Ticket:

"Turn them in by the end of the day," she said, and walked away with Victoria. "Come on, Victoria. Let's decide what to wear to the concert."

Mara crumpled up her paper and walked away.

Phillip held his in front of him and pretended like he was going to throw up on it. Resa and I laughed, and then Resa folded her paper into an airplane and sailed it toward a recycling bin. It missed.

"I can't even get lucky at that," she said, and went to get it.

Saki, Natalie, Pablo, and Riley got up to go back to their practice. "If our video doesn't win," Saki said, "I hope yours does."

"Back at you," Phillip said.

Recess ended, and then we had to get through the afternoon. Finally, school was out.

"Showtime!" Phillip said.

The three of us grabbed our ukes and met by the picnic table. We practiced a bunch of times and decided where to stand. Then Phillip propped up his cell phone on the table, pushed RECORD, and we sang and played for real.

Sun without warning.
Sun in the morning.
Sun dancing through my window pane.

Peace without warning.
Peace in the morning.
Peace back to say hello, my friend.

After all these trips and
falls,
I'm gonna get up, gonna
gonna get up again.

The first verses were perfect. We smiled at each other and kept singing the other verses. We were sounding great! We went through the whole song and got to the end without a single mistake.

"We nailed it!" Resa said.

The three of us started jumping up and down.

"Let's watch it," Phillip said, and we gathered around his cell phone. He pressed the PLAY button. "Ta-da!"

There were our feet. You could hear us singing, but all you could see was our feet for the whole video.

"We should've played the ukes with our toes instead of our fingers," Resa said.

"My fault," Phillip said. "Sorry. We have to do it again."

We did it again and this time it was all sky.

"It's too hard to get it right without holding the phone," Phillip moaned.

"I have an idea," Resa said. "Why don't we make three videos? One of each of us. We can hold the phone for each other and get it just right."

"But then we'll be competing against each other," I said.

"As long as we all promise to invite each other if we win, we'll be okay," she said.

Phillip nodded. "This will actually increase our chances. Great idea, Resa."

I held the phone for Phillip's video, and we both cheered him on. Phillip held the phone for Resa, and we cheered her on. And then Resa held the phone for me, and they both cheered me on.

"That was fun," Phillip said. "And now we have three excellent videos. I'll send you each your video. Get your parents to submit it."

We did a triple fist bump again.

"Now for my big surprise," Resa said. "I brought a reward for when we got done!"

She pulled a big bag of potato chips from her backpack.

"Salty, crunchy, lovely potato chips! I love you!" I yelled, and hugged the bag.

"No crushing!" Phillip said,
and pulled them away.
We chowed down.
Crunch. Crunch. Munch.

Chapter Eighteen

HIDE AND SEEK?
HIDE AND PEEK!

On my way home, I passed by Scarlett's house and heard voices. *She and Victoria must be making their video in Scarlett's backyard,* I thought. And then I couldn't stop wondering how it was going. Quietly, I crept around the side of Scarlett's house and hid behind a big flowering bush. I peeked out.

Scarlett and Victoria had made a kind of curtain by hanging a sheet on the shed, and they were singing and playing their ukuleles in front of it. And they had makeup on! Lots of it. All over their cheeks and eyes. They even had on lipstick!

Brandy, Scarlett's little sister, was sitting in a chair holding up a cell phone, so that meant they couldn't get the fancy video camera after all.

"Stop!" Scarlett yelled.

"Why?" Victoria screamed. "We were almost done!"

"I want this to be good," Scarlett said. "Don't you?"

"It was good!"

"It wasn't right," Scarlett said. "We weren't together. And you were singing a little too loud."

"I was not!" Victoria said.

"You couldn't hear yourself because you were too loud," Scarlett said. "Trust me."

"Well, you rubbed your eye in the middle of it," Victoria said. "That looked bad."

"I did not!"

"You did, too. You just said your eyes feel itchy."

Brandy laughed.

"Don't film this!" Scarlett yelled.

"It's funny," Brandy said. "I'm going to post it."

"Delete that right now!" Scarlett said, and grabbed the phone.

"Give me my dollar now," Brandy said. "This is annoying."

"No!" Scarlett snapped. "I told you I'd give you a dollar when we're done, and we're not done!"

In a way, it was lucky that I heard those voices and came over to spy because I was seeing something important. I shouldn't be jealous of Scarlett. Nobody here was having any fun. And having fun with friends is the best. My friends and I had a blast together today, and Scarlett and Victoria missed out.

Carefully, I turned to leave and stepped on a stick.

"What was that?" Scarlett said.

I froze.

Then from one of the flowers on the bush, a huge bee flew out and hovered right in front of my face.

"Yikes!" I screamed, and jumped out.

"Lucy McGee?"

"A bee!" I yelled, and ran.

I heard Scarlett yelling behind me. "Lucy McGee, were you spying on us?"

"Who, me?" I yelled back.

Chapter Nineteen

DON'T YOU HATE TO WAIT?

Entering a contest is both fun and not fun. Until it's over your brain bounces between "maybe I'll win" and "maybe I'll lose." After my parents entered my video that Thursday my brain was playing ping-pong all night long.

The next day Resa and I got to school at the same

time. Phillip was waiting by the fence, chewing his thumbnail.

"Guys, guess who else entered the give-away?" he asked.

"Mr. Chomper?" Resa asked.

"Ha ha," Phillip said.

"The queen of England?" Resa asked.

"No!" Phillip said. "Actually, I don't know. Maybe. But I doubt it. Stop guessing! I'll tell you." He paused for dramatic effect. "Jeremy Bing!"

"Jeremy Bing doesn't even like Ben & Bree," Resa said.

"I know!" Phillip said. "He just told me he entered because he likes to win free things. He said if he wins he's going to sell the tickets and put the money in the bank."

"This is not a good sign," I said. "I bet a million people entered."

Ben & Bree were going to announce the winner at six o'clock tonight, which meant we had to get through the day. And it was just starting.

Just then Scarlett showed up wearing big movie-star sunglasses. I thought she was going to brag about how great she looked with all that makeup on in her video, but she just walked by.

Victoria and a bunch of girls were standing by the doors, but Scarlett walked over to the Buddy Bench and sat down. At our school, the Buddy Bench is where you can sit if you are sad. If you see someone sit on the Buddy Bench, you're supposed to go over and cheer them up.

"Are you seeing what I'm seeing?" Resa asked.

"Scarlett Tandy has never in her entire life sat on the Buddy Bench," Phillip said.

The three of us walked over. By the time we got there, the rest of the Songwriting Club had noticed and had come over, too.

"What's wrong, Scarlett?" Victoria asked.

She took off her sunglasses. Her face was red and puffy! She didn't look like Scarlett. She looked like a tomato with sad eyes.

"I put on my mom's makeup without permission. And after Victoria left, I broke out in hives." She sniffed. "I'm allergic to makeup."

We were all quiet. Then there was a sad little sound of gulping. She was trying not to cry.

She went on. "My dad got so mad, he sold the tickets to the Ben & Bree Show. And he said even if I win the giveaway, I can't go."

Nobody knew what to say.

Finally, Resa asked, "Does it still itch?"

Scarlett nodded.

"We're all really sorry for you, Scarlett," Saki said. "Right?"

Everybody nodded.

"You're not mad at me anymore, Mara?" Scarlett asked.

Mara shrugged. "Kind of. But it's hard to be really mad at somebody who looks as itchy as you."

"Thank you," Scarlett said. She tried to smile, which made her face look like a squashed tomato, and then she pulled a stack of papers out of her backpack. "I made all of you one of these," she said, and handed us each one.

JUST IN CASE

If you win the giveaway, please feel sorry for me and give just one of your extra tickets to me. Then ask your mom or dad to call my dad and talk him into letting me go. I think my dad will listen to another grown-up.

If you do this, you can pick one of these thank-you gifts:

- I'll give you two brand-new glitter pens.
- You can have anything from my lunch for one week.
- You can keep your favorite of my necklaces or earrings (but don't tell your parents or my parents).

- If you're in Mrs. Brock's class, I'll clean Mr. Chomper's cage when it's your turn.
- I will say nice things about how you look every day for two weeks.
- I'll give you my allowance for one whole month.

Nobody said anything. Then the whistle blew for school to start. We stuffed the notes in our backpacks and headed inside.

On the way Resa whispered to me and Phillip. "Hey, when I brought those potato chips yesterday, did it feel like I was trying to buy your friendship?"

"No!" I said. "That was just a nice surprise."

"Yeah," Phillip said. "Do not hesitate to bring us potato chips. Ever."

Resa laughed.

"I hope I never have to buy my friends," Phillip added. "'Cause I got nothing."

"Guys," I said. "At six o'clock we'll find out if we're winners or losers. If we win, how will we ever decide who to give our extra ticket to?"

Phillip shook his head. "I'm not even going to think about it."

"Let's just see if we win," Resa said.

I nodded. One step at a time. I just wanted time to go a lot faster!

Chapter Twenty

─ TICKTOCK, SIX O'CLOCK ─

Bong! Bong! Bong! Bong! Bong! Bong!

Finally, the moment of truth.

I was in the middle of eating leftover tofu taco pie with my family when the clock struck six.

"It's time!" I jumped up. "We have to check the contest!"

My mom pulled out her cell phone, and I raced over. She opened up her app and started scrolling through the messages.

"Do a hashtag search," I said, and closed my eyes. "I can't look!"

"Hold on. There's a lot about Ben & Bree," my mom said.

My dad pulled out his phone and started searching, too.

Please let it be me, I chanted. *Please let it be me. Please let it be me.*

Or Phillip. Or Resa. Or at least not Scarlett.

"Here it is!" my mom said, and then she read the tweet out loud. "Thanks to all our fans. Winner of the tickets giveaway is . . . Nico Pasi. Congrats, Nico!"

"Nico Pasi?" I cried. "Who is that?" My heart thudded.

"I'm sorry, honey," my mom said.

"You gave it a good try," my dad said.

I kind of wanted to cry, but I didn't want to seem like a baby. "It's okay," I said. "Lucy No Prize McGee. That's me."

"Oh, Lucy!" my mom said.

While we finished dinner, I thought about my friends and Mr. Tapper and even Jeremy Bing. Everybody was probably having a sad night.

"Bo?" Lily asked.

"You can ride in the boat first, Lucy," Leo said. "I'll push."

They were trying to cheer me up. "No thanks," I said. "I'm just going to go up to my room and feel sorry for myself for a while."

Sometimes you gotta do what you gotta do.

I was busy lying on my bed staring at the ceiling when there was a knock on my door.

My dad, mom, Leo, and Lily all came in.

Leo and Lily jumped on my bed and snuggled in. Then my mom and dad both joined in, too. It was a squash.

"We missed you, Lucy," my mom said.

"And we have an idea," my dad said.

"We know how disappointed you and your friends are not to be able to go to the concert," my mom said. "So we thought you and your Songwriting Club could put on your own concert here tomorrow night."

"We could have a party and invite the kids and their parents, and you guys could sing for us," my dad said. "We've been meaning to have a potluck for everybody in the club."

"You mean a pity party?" I asked.

My parents laughed. "A real party," my dad said.

Leo exclaimed, "And it isn't even anybody's birthday."

"We can invite everybody in the Songwriting Club?" I asked.

"Sure. It's a potluck," my mom said. "That means we don't have to cook everything."

"Actually," my dad said. "We *need* to invite everybody. We don't want any hard feelings. We can send everybody an e-mail or a text."

"Can we invite Ms. Adamson and Mr. Tapper, too?"

"The more the merrier," my mom said. "But it's short notice, Lucy, so not everybody will be able to come."

"I know! But whoever can come is going to be so happy!" I said. "All because of us! Thank you!"

I don't think Lily knew  what was going on, but she squealed and threw her pacifier in the air, and then we had a very squashy group hug.

Chapter Twenty-One

FOOD AND FRIENDS TO THE END?

On Saturday we decorated the backyard with a string of twinkle lights (my idea!) and put a big sign on the door that said FREE CONCERT IN THE BACKYARD (my idea!) and made popcorn (Leo's idea!), and people started coming. It wasn't dark yet, so you couldn't really see the lights, but it still looked nice.

When you're used to seeing people only at school, it makes you nervous at first to see them hanging around your own backyard, but then you get used to it and it's fun. Scarlett came, and her tomato face looked better. She wasn't even bossy. She was just happy to be included.

My dad fired up the grill, and everybody brought tons of food and set it out on the picnic table. All the grown-ups kept talking and talking, and so we decided to grab plates and get started.

"Are you thinking what I'm thinking?" Pablo asked as he took a plate.

"What are you thinking?" Phillip asked.

"Dessert first?" He smiled.

We all stuffed our faces with cookies, cake, lasagna, tamales, sesame noodles, and salad, and the grown-ups didn't even notice.

Then Ms. Adamson walked in with her ukulele and . . . a man! He had a long beard and a guitar!

"I think that's her boyfriend," Phillip whispered.

"I hope they get married and ask us to play in their wedding," Resa whispered.

"Hi everybody," she said. "This is my friend Jason. Jason, this is the famous Songwriting Club I've been telling you about!"

Phillip stood up and bowed, and we all laughed.

"We thought we could jam together after the concert," Ms. Adamson said.

Then Mr. Tapper appeared, carrying a big drum. "Hey! Hey! This must be where the party's at!" He shook my dad and mom's hands, and then he walked over and fist-bumped Ms. Adamson and Jason and all of us. He had brought a friend, too, who also had a drum.

It started to get dark, and the twinkle lights started shining.

"Let's have a toast," Resa said.

All my friends lifted up their cups. "I really wanted to see Ben & Bree," Phillip said. "But this party was a good idea."

"Thanks for inviting
all of us, Lucy," Mara said.

Everybody said thanks, and we
all clinked our cups. When people
clink your cup, it makes you feel
happy on the outside and inside.

"Come on," Saki said. "Let's do
the concert!"

We got our ukes and tuned up in the front
yard.

"I think you should stand in the middle and

introduce us," Natalie said to me. "Because it's your party, Lucy."

We practiced a few times, and then we went into the backyard and announced that we were ready.

The grown-ups moved all the chairs to the grass, and we stood on the patio facing them like we were on a stage.

"Welcome to the Songwriting Club Concert," I said. "We are going to sing three songs for you. One is a Ben & Bree song. We still like them even though they didn't pick us to go to their concert."

Everybody laughed.

"The other two songs are ones we wrote."

"Because we are the Songwriting Club," Phillip said. "That's what we do."

Everybody laughed again.

"Ready?" I looked at all my friends.

Everybody was smiling. The sky above us
was dark now, which made the string of lights
sparkle in the prettiest way. Everything was

perfect. My stomach was full of good food. My
lost uke was back in my arms. My brain didn't
have a single worry. We sang:

Love in my corner.
Love feeling warmer.
Love back to say hello, my friend.

After all these trips and falls,
   I'm gonna get up, gonna gonna get up
again.

I'm sure the Ben & Bree concert that night was great. But ours was great, too, and it was free!

Lucky me, Lucy McGee!

THE SONGWRITING CLUB SONGS

Have fun with the songs
in this book. You can hear
the songs and sing along
by going to the special
Lucy page on my site:
www.maryamato.com/
lucy-songs/.

You can also find out more
about making up your own
songs and learning how to play
songs on a ukulele, piano, or
guitar.

TWO BRAINS

I've got two brains in my mixed-up head.
They don't get along. They fight instead.
One says yes and the other says no.
One says fast and the other says slow.
One hates my guts and the other thinks I'm fine.
I want to trade them in for a brand-new mind.

PITY PARTY

I'm a loser. I got no luck.
When a bird flies by, I forget to duck.

Four-leaf clover? Just makes me sneeze.
Cough near me, I'll get a disease.

Come to my pity party, please, oh please.
Come to my pity party, please.

If it rains on my house, expect a flood.
At the end of my rainbow is a pot of mud.

Lucky ladybugs hide when I appear.
If I see a bee, it'll sting my rear.

Come to my pity party, please, oh please.
Come to my pity party, please.

When I cross my fingers, all I get is an ache.
If I drop something fancy, it's gonna break.

My genie in a bottle? Got shipped to France.
I get no prize when the game is chance.

Come to my pity party, please, oh please.
Come to my pity party, please.

I'm sad and squashed like a poor, ugly bug.
What I need right now is an itty-bitty hug.

Come to my pity party, please, oh please.
Come to my pity party, please.

GET UP
(BEN & BREE'S SONG)

Sun without warning.
Sun in the morning.
Sun dancing through my window pane.

Peace without warning.
Peace in the morning.
Peace back to say hello, my friend.

After all these trips and falls,
I'm gonna get up, gonna gonna get up again.

Time in my corner.
Time feeling warmer.
Time just to stretch and breathe and bend.

Light in my corner.
Light feeling warmer.
Light at this long, dark tunnel's end.

After all these trips and falls,
I'm gonna get up, gonna gonna get up,
Gonna get up, gonna gonna get up again.

Joy without warning.
Joy in the morning.
Joy dancing through my window pane.

Love in my corner.
Love feeling warmer.
Love back to say hello, my friend.

After all these trips and falls,
I'm gonna get up, gonna gonna get up,
Gonna get up, gonna gonna get up,
Gonna gonna get, gonna get,
gonna get up again.

SING ALONG WITH MORE LUCY MCGEE ADVENTURES!

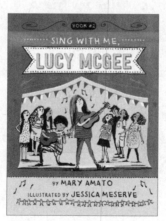

A STAR ON TV,

LUCY MCGEE

Read a sneak
peek from
Lucy's next
adventure. . . .

Chapter One

I hate wet socks. When it's raining and you can't find your rain boots, you have to be careful walking to school.

Today there were puddles everywhere. By the time I got to the end of my street, I had hopped over seven big ones. Only two blocks more to get to my school. So far so good. My dad was way behind me with Leo and Lily and the big black umbrella. They were walking super slow because my little brother, Leo, had to name every worm he saw on the sidewalk.

Wumpy, Chumpy, Humpy, Dumpy . . . Leo is excellent at names.

I walked ahead with my blue umbrella in one hand and my ukulele in the other. I turned the corner. *Whoa!* Right in front of the sidewalk heading into school was the biggest puddle of all. It was deep and wide and long and muddy.

I crouched down and got all my energy ready. I leaped! I soared! My feet lifted into the air and landed . . . *plop!* Right in the middle.

Disgusting.

I turned back and saw a red umbrella with legs and a ukulele poking out from under it heading for the same puddle. I knew those legs. I knew that ukulele. It was my friend Phillip Lee.

"Watch out!" I yelled, just as Phillip tried to hop over the puddle.

He landed in the middle. "Lucy! I hate wet socks."

"Me too," I said.

He walked toward me, water oozing out of his shoes.

"Well, you know what they say?" I asked.

He shrugged. "When life gives you lemons, make lemonade?"

"When life gives you wet socks, sing about it!" I
said, and started to make up a song:

It drizzled all night
and it's pouring right now.
You think it's raining cats and dogs?
I'd say it's raining . . . cows!

Before you leave the house,
pack an extra pair of socks,
especially if you have to walk
a couple of blocks.

Phillip laughed. He added to the song:

The puddles are so deep
they're probably filled with fish.
When you step in a puddle
your shoes go . . . squish.

"We got the rhymes!" I said. "Now it's finish time."
I sang:

So pack that extra pair
of socks for your feet.
Your toes will thank you
and think you're sweet.

Phillip tried to clap, which was hard because he was holding his umbrella.

We sang the song again. Another umbrella with legs stopped to listen.

"Great song!" The umbrella lifted up. It was Pablo.

As we walked into the school together, Pablo said, "Hey, I've got an idea. It's my turn to read the weather report on *The Morning Mix*. Teach me the song, and we'll sing it together on the show. Your song is way better than what I was going to read."

I started jumping up and down, my wet shoes landing with a *squish, squish*. Being on our school's morning TV show is so fun. Only fifth graders get to do the show. Fourth graders like us can only be on as special guests.

"We have to hurry," Pablo said. "Get your teacher's permission and come to the Media Center. And bring your ukes!"

Pablo headed down the fifth-grade hall toward the Media Center.

"I'm glad our feet got wet," Phillip said. "I think it's destiny."

Just then I heard a familiar sound coming down the hallway.

Clack, clack, clack.

I pulled Phillip behind Mr. Tapper's big rolling garbage bin.

"What are we doing?" Phillip asked.

"Shh! We're hiding."

I crouched down.

"Why?" he whispered, and crouched down next to me.

"Listen . . ."

Clack, clack, clack.

We peeked out. Scarlett Tandy was coming. Scarlett is a friend of ours and she's also in the Songwriting Club, which Phillip started. She can be fun, but she can also be a tornado of trouble. If Scarlett found out what we wanted to do, I was afraid she would make herself the star. I just wanted to keep it simple.

I crossed my fingers and hoped she didn't see us.

Chapter Two

Hiding behind a garbage bin is hard enough. Hiding behind it when you're dripping wet and you have a backpack and a ukulele and an umbrella, and you have to sneeze, is even worse. I pinched my nose to keep from sneezing and we waited.

Clack, clack, clack. Scarlett's shoes were coming. Of course Scarlett's shoes didn't go *squish, squish, squish*. Even though she lives next to the school, her parents drive her whenever it rains.

The sound was getting closer and closer and my nose was

getting ticklier and ticklier. And then Phillip's eyes got huge. He pointed at my foot. I looked down.

Wriggling around on the tip of my shoe was a worm!

Phillip started to laugh, picked up the worm, and dangled it in front of my face, which made me want to laugh. My laugh and my sneeze came out in one big *"Haha-achoo!"*

Scarlett heard. "What are you two doing back here?"

Phillip looked at me. "What are we doing, Lucy?"

"Nothing. We're just hanging out with our new friend Wumpy," I said, and held up the worm.

"Ew!" Scarlett yelled as she *clack, clack, clack*ed away. "You guys are disgusting!"

Phillip and I stood up.

"Was that mean of me?" I asked him. "I just think that if Scarlett knows what we're doing, something bad will happen."

He shrugged. "She always wants to be the boss of everything. It's a problem." Then he gave me one of his looks. "But she's going to find out."

"Let's not go to our classroom. Let's just go to the Media Center and do it!" I said. "We're studying weather in science now, Phillip. Mrs. Brock will love our idea. Once she sees us on TV, she'll be so proud of us she won't care!"

Phillip shook his head. "No way. We need permission. Even if it means Scarlett finds out. Come on or Mrs. Brock will think we're absent. Bring Wumpy along and we can put her in Mrs. Brock's ivy plant."

I looked at Phillip. He just didn't understand. I had to take control, but how? And then a sneaky idea popped into my head.

"I've got it!" I said. "I know a way to tell Mrs. Brock what we want to do without Scarlett finding out! I'll take care of Mrs. Brock. You go to the Media Center and tell Ms. Dell that I'm coming."

"What if Mrs. Brock says no?"

"She won't! See you in a minute."

I put Wumpy in my pocket and headed toward our classroom. When I was outside the door, I set down my stuff and got out a piece of paper and a pencil.

Dear Mrs. Brock,

*There is an emergency. Phillip and
I must sing the weather report on The
Morning Mix. We will be a little late to
class, but it will be worth it. This is our
duty.*

Your helpful student,
Lucy McGee

I folded up the paper. Then I peeked into the classroom. Everybody was putting stuff in their cubbies.

I slipped the paper under the door and walked as quickly as possible to the Media Center. Mrs. Brock would see the note and be happy that two of her students were being creative and helpful. What could go wrong?